Yo-bot, the Classroom Robot

Story by Cameron Macintosh
Illustrations by Sumiti Collina

Contents

Chapter 1

A New Helper

As the children of class 2D walked into the classroom on Monday morning, their eyes grew wide.

There was something strange in the middle of the room. It was about as high as a small boy or girl, but there was a sheet over the top of it.

"What is under that sheet?" asked Kain.

"A very nice surprise!" answered Ms Devi.

When everyone sat down, Ms Devi said,
"Say hello to my wonderful new helper!"

Ms Devi took the sheet away.

The children gasped.
Standing in front of them was a robot.
It was made of plastic and golden metal.

"This robot will be here all week," said Ms Devi.
"He will help me during your lessons.
He can talk, and he is very good at yoga!"

"Does he have a name?" asked Jin.

"Not yet," said Ms Devi.
"I need you all to decide on a name for him."

"I have an idea," said Zara.
"He is good at yoga, so why don't we call him Yo-bot?"

Everyone thought Yo-bot was a great name for the robot.

That afternoon, Ms Devi sat at the back of the room as Yo-bot gave the class a yoga lesson. Everyone followed the poses he showed them. Yo-bot was a very good yoga teacher!

The next day, Yo-bot gave the class
another yoga lesson.
It was a lot of fun.
All of the children looked forward to their next lesson.

Chapter 2

A Loud Crackle

On Wednesday, Yo-bot was showing the class
a new yoga pose.
Suddenly, he started bouncing up and down.
The children bounced up and down, too.

Yo-bot kept on bouncing for a long time.

At last, Ali said, “Is something the matter with Yo-bot?”

Just then, there was a loud crackle
and a puff of smoke came out of the top of Yo-bot’s head.
He seemed to lose his balance,
and then he flopped onto the table with a crash.

"Oh, no!" cried Lola. "I think we've hurt Yo-bot. We've made him do too much yoga."

Ms Devi hurried over and looked at Yo-bot.

"You did not hurt Yo-bot," she said,
"but I'm afraid I'll have to phone the robot doctor to come and fix him."

Chapter 3

Yoga Without Yo-bot

Later that day, the robot doctor came and took Yo-bot away.

"I hope Yo-bot will be all right," said Ali, looking disappointed.

"I hope so, too," said Ms Devi.

"How will we do our yoga now?" asked Julia.

"I can remember one of the poses Yo-bot showed us," said Sienna, grinning.
"I'll stand at the front and show everyone!"

"That's a great idea," said Ms Devi.
"Anyone who remembers a pose can have a turn at leading the class while Yo-bot is away."

The next day, Sienna was the first to lead the class in a yoga pose.
Everyone joined in.

Then, Julia led the class in another pose.

Most of the other children had a turn, too.

"Well done, class," said Ms Devi.
"You can all do yoga very well without Yo-bot!"

Chapter 4

A Friend Comes Back

On Friday, as the class was doing yoga together, there was a knock on the door.

Ms Devi opened the door.

The robot doctor had brought Yo-bot back!
"I have fixed your robot already!"
the doctor said to everyone.

Ms Devi picked Yo-bot up and put him on her desk. Yo-bot waved and said hello to everyone.

"It's great to see you again, Yo-bot," said Kain. "I'm very glad you are feeling better!"

"We can do our yoga on our own now,"
Jin said to Yo-bot.
"But you can watch us, and join in, too!"